WHAT JOHNNO DID NEXT ...

A cautionary tale for the ages

Dr X

To find out more about this book, or to contact the author, please visit: www.vividpublishing.com.au/drx

Copyright © 2014 Fingerprint Communications NSW Pty Ltd (Australia)

Published by Vivid Publishing
P.O. Box 948, Fremantle
Western Australia 6959
www.vividpublishing.com.au

National Library of Australia cataloguing-in-publication data:
Creator: Dr. X, author.
Title: What Johnno did next / Dr X.
ISBN: 9781925209389 (paperback)
Subjects: Hope--Fiction.
Dewey Number: A823.4

Dedication

*Because people are more important
than shovels.*

This is a story that happens not far from where you are right now. Just there, near the horizon …

Chapter 1

Things Were Grim

Things were grim in Grimsby. Even the grass struggled. But that was nothing compared to when people's legs started shrinking. The ones they called SLAKARS. The ones who thought it wouldn't matter so much, given the way the world was going. That's when the real trouble started.

And so we must begin – not far from here – at the home of Alistair Farquhar 'The Fourth'.

He was a nice enough boy, and would have been even nicer in a different family. He was respectful, clean-cut, and fairly good looking. The other kids called him 'the mannequin'. But all things considered, a pretty decent fellow.

The problem was he only knew what he

knew. And what he knew was *The Bat & Ball Company* was a good place, because that's what his parents told him. And from his parents' point of view, it *was* a good place. Because they owned *The Bat & Ball Company* and it made them very rich indeed.

Alistair's father (who was also called Alistair, but was known in his family as 'The Third'), was in all the business magazines. They said he was a great success. He'd shut down the local factory, the one his grandfather started 100 years ago, and moved the whole thing to the remote country of Fahraysha. It just so happened that this new location was packed with eager workers and most of them were poor.

The business magazines used plenty of big words to explain why moving the company was so clever. Words like 'globalisation'.

But what it really came down to, was The Third didn't have to pay his Fahraysha workers as much as the Grimbsy ones. And because he didn't need to pay the new workers so much, it meant Alistair's family got to keep more money for themselves. Alistair's parents said it was a good thing, because they were giving jobs to poor people. And they were right.

But things were different in Lower Grimsby, home to recent teen Johnny Harrison – a mess of strawberry blond hair, smiling sky blue eyes, and with that certain something about him.

His dad, Horrie, used to work at the original factory, checking to see all the bats and balls were OK before they got sent to the shops. Horrie was very popular with the other workers. He was a cheery, lanky fellow with a lick of brownish, reddish hair. The factory was a friendly, happy place, with Horrie at the centre of the action in his bib 'n brace overalls. He would even give a wink and let them 'test' the gear in their lunchbreak, before the trucks left. It became known as the Quality Control Cup, and they had a trophy for it.

As Horrie would explain: "We need to know our gear will stand up to a right proper game lad. It's all about quality and reputation – 'cause if you haven't got a good name, you've got nothing much at all."

The children of the workers and managers also came round after school and were

allowed to play with the gear (for reputation's sake of course). Horrie stuck an
old ball on a block of wood and covered it
in gold paint. So the kids had their own
competition as well – for 'The Golden Orb'.

Then it was back home to the smells of
bread and cakes, a crackling warm fire,
and the most delicious casseroles and
stews tempting everyone ahead of dinner-
time. And around the table the heaving,
rolling laughter as the great yarns of the
day grew longer by the moment.

Until one day.

While the Quality Control Cup was being
fought out amongst the workers, Horrie's
heart skipped a beat. A burst of adrenalin
surged through his body. His eyes could
not believe what they were taking in.

A 'world exclusive' in the Grimsby
Gazette, by cub reporter Ophelia Payne,
revealed the factory was going to shut
down.

In the article, an expert said it was an
especially clever move to shift the factory,
because the recently elected government
had made a trade deal with Fahraysha. It
was all part of the *'Expanding Our Horizons
– Making Life Cheap'* election commitment

and meant people would get cheaper things. Plus, it meant the government would pay to move all the *Bat & Ball* machines to the new country, without Alistair's family having to pay a cent.

But Horrie Harrison didn't think it was particularly clever at all. "Trade deal my pipe!" he blurted, with the veins in his neck sticking out like small mountain ridges. "What they've traded is our bleedin' jobs, and our bleedin' hopes and dreams – right down to the cheapest bidder." And he was right.

It meant the Farquhars and the Harrisons would lead very different lives, but they do cross paths again in a most unexpected way. Because the Farquhars kept living in Grimsby, although for Alistair's parents it was more of a 'home base' (which will be explained in a bit more detail later on). And they were always using their computers to check in with the new managers at the Fahraysha factory, to make sure they were making as much money as possible.

They also put up a big fence around their house, with security cameras on the corners, as well as installing a lovely heated swimming pool inside their compound.

While the construction was going on, there was a farewell party at the factory. As the evening wore on, everyone got a bit emotional. Some cried, some got angry, and Horrie seemed to take an increasing interest in macroeconomics.

"There's no such bleedin' thing as a global economy!" he enlightened, and everyone agreed with him even before he'd finished making his case.

"It's the intestine economy we live in." (For some reason everyone kept nodding.)

"That's why the economy was invented in the first place – to feed ourselves. But it's all gone a bit gutless now."

The factory farewell ended with the final staging of the Quality Control Cup. There was a lot of joking and laughing and it didn't really matter who won. But afterwards the other workers presented Horrie with the Cup, and told him it was his to keep.

Horrie tried to speak to say thanks, but no words came out, so everyone just hugged and cried and laughed. Eventually people started drifting away, saying they'd all stay in touch. But drift away they did.

The next day, there was no place for

Horrie to go – so he just stayed in bed, and pretended (rather unconvincingly) that it was a great treat. "Oh, it's like bein' on 'oliday," he declared. But for the most part, he didn't venture out or say much at all.

For when Horrie Harrison lost his job, Johnny's world changed forever.

And as you're about to discover, it was a terrible almost hopeless time – for a very long time – before events would change everything, in the most incredible way.

But even when things seemed at their worst, Johnny always remembered his mother's favourite saying.

Wiping her hands on her tattered old apron, and with her light hair looking a little messy from all the cleaning work she did around Grimsby, Jenny Harrison would smile at Johnny and say: "A ray of hope burns brightest in the darkest places."

Then she'd pause and say: "So always keep your heart burning bright darling boy – keep your heart burning bright."

Johnny would later recall that – when she said those words – she was the most beautiful and wisest person in the world, all at the same time.

Chapter 2

Pressure and Payne

There was a time when *The Bat & Ball Company* wasn't the only factory in town. In fact, Grimsby was full of them, and they made all manner of things. But mostly they made black smoke.

Back then, the world came to town – looking for work in the factories – and the Smiths and the Joneses started to mix with the Polanskis and the Chengs, the Russos and the Garcias.

The council at the time had the good sense to run a campaign called *"Grimsby: We're All In This Together"*. As part of the program, there was a free dance in the town square every Friday night. For the most part, people came together and laughed and talked and got to know each other and found they had far more in common than they realised. And the world was a richer place for it.

Later, when governments changed the rules and the factories closed, many of these same people would be forced to move on, looking for a job and a better life. But back when all the factories were running, anything seemed possible. Hope could be realised.

It was just such a lure that brought Ophelia Payne's parents to Grimsby, when she was only a baby. They were chasing hope out of fear. And even though she became a great newspaper reporter, she never got to know her own history all that well – at least, not while her parents were alive (but that's a whole other story).

Her parents simply didn't want to talk about the dangers, and the anguish of the place they left behind. It made them too upset just talking about it. Sometimes you sensed a glint of fear in their eyes. There was even a suggestion the family surname had been changed when they came to Grimsby, just in case the nightmare followed them to this new place and gave them trouble like before. So, out of love,

Ophelia always curbed her instincts to find out more and let them be. And they set about enjoying the life they now had.

But it stirred something in her. The desire to know and understand, to explain and to help. For Ophelia growing up, she wanted to learn the stories of the amazing people she found around her. For while she may have had a disarming pixie-like look to her, she had a driving curiosity. It was something made all the more effective and potent, when combined with the fight and determination of a terrier.

Ophelia's parents worked three jobs each, putting their daughter through Grimsby Grammar, where she landed a role on the school newspaper, *The Pupil's Pimpernel*, and immediately got down to business.

To start with, she profiled the lives of teachers and cleaners, eventually working her way up to the big exclusives. Such as the controversy surrounding the disappearing cream buns in the tuckshop – an exposé which saw the school get a new canteen lady.

One special investigation led to another, till she finally found herself on a collision course with the head of English, Nicholas Nicholby.

Ophelia had been motivated to act, when she realised most of her fellow students could send a *txt 2u* but couldn't string a basic sentence together – leaving them with dim prospects for the rest of their lives.

Her headline exclaimed "2B OR NOT 2B – THIS 8NT ENGLISH!" and her story opened with this explosive paragraph:

The English Department at this, and other schools, stands accused of failing to deliver good grammar skills to its students and, instead, dressing up Literature as the cornerstone for the subject – which it clearly is not.

The story noted Nicholas Nicholby had failed to return *The Pimpernel's* calls before deadline, and that any grammatical errors in the report should be blamed on the English department for failing to teach Ophelia, the daughter of immigrants, how to write properly.

Rather than just being an opinion piece though, Ophelia had approached leading authors and retired educators, seeking their opinions on whether English should be about learning to spell, write and read, or being able to explain the meaning of stories. Most of them, even the authors, said that writing and reading should come first, and the meaning of stories after.

It's fair to say the exclusive was controversial. It got picked up by the main local paper, the Grimsby Gazette, and then went right across the country in The National Times. Before you knew it, the story was being fiercely debated on television and radio, and Ophelia was in the headmaster's office with her parents.

Fortunately the headmaster was of the wise-and-well-connected variety, and agreement was struck for Ophelia to channel her skills and energy into a work placement program at the Grimsby Gazette, on the understanding that she would give up her role on *The Pimpernel*, allowing some other hopeful to hone their skills. Everyone was exceedingly happy with the arrangement.

And so began a career, which before too long, would break one of the biggest stories ever known.

Chapter 3
Reality Bites

The Quality Control Cup sat on the window-sill, where the rest of the world (and Horrie) could see it. Horrie asked his wife that it not be touched, and she knew from the emotional crack in his voice not to ask why and left it well alone. It started off very shiny, but after a few weeks the Cup started looking dusty and dull.

The whole house felt weighed down by deep sadness. Horrie didn't say much at all, and said less each passing day, despite Johnny's best efforts to fire up a conversation. Johnny had to go to school most days, and often returned to find his Dad sitting in the very same chair he'd been in that morning. Horrie would muster up a smile and try to give Johnny a wink, but his eyes didn't have their normal sparkle.

Occasionally, when he did speak, he'd often say the same thing. "Remember my boy that people are more important than shovels. Always have been, always will be." And, of course, he was right.

Every so often his lip would quiver as he stared blankly out the window, and the silence would come back and just hang there. How they all hated that silence.

It was like a slow relentless ache that wouldn't go away.

Johnny felt he understood the shovel message, but he hoped his dad would get another job soon enough and find new workmates to laugh with. He was used to having great conversations with Horrie about football and places to explore. He missed that for himself, but mostly he just wanted his Dad to be happy.

But something else started to happen around this time. Johnny noticed his Mum had been crying a lot. She tried to hide it, but he could tell.

Jenny Harrison used to clean houses in the area, and now that Horrie had lost his job she was the only one making any new money for food and bills. But a lot of the people she used to clean for had also lost their jobs when the factory closed. So they couldn't keep her on.

Soon she had only a few jobs left, and a dark cloud descended on the Harrison household. It was becoming obvious they couldn't afford to stay there much longer (but they couldn't afford to go anywhere else either).

Jenny's hand started to tremble at times, leaving Johnny feeling hopeless, confused and scared. Sometimes his stomach would be gripped by a painful cold flash, like an icy hand grabbing deep inside him and squeezing.

But despite the darkness and the chill descending into their lives – or maybe because of it – a spark was lit. Johnny understood, quite simply, that he had to do *something*.

What had begun to eat at him, soon began to burn in him. Not an anger, but a steely determination. A drive with what felt like an endless supply of fuel.

At one time it would have seemed brave, but now it was straight forward. Johnny made a pact with himself. A personal mission – to seek out answers.

He didn't quite know how he could possibly put things right, but he knew he had to at least try to make things better. On his own, in the background, causing no upset, making no fuss. Inviting no critics to derail his efforts and, ultimately, delivering something positive.

The switch had been flicked. It was time to get moving.

The Harrisons didn't have a car, but Johnny did have the *Red Rocket*. (That was his name for the rusty old bike he'd reefed out of the weeds near the back fence, and painted fire engine red.)

And because the Harrisons also didn't own a computer, there was one place Johnny had to go. The Library.

Johnny later realised it was an incredible piece of luck that they didn't own a car or a computer, especially when it came to the people developing short legs. It was also quite lucky Johnny had the Red Rocket, because he got even more exercise than a normal bike – straining to push its rusty old pedals around.

The Red Rocket and Johnny would have many great adventures and plenty of thrilling close calls (but that's a whole other story). For right now, with a driven focus, Johnny was embarking on his mission.

At the library they had a computer you could use for free, for 20 minutes at a time. But even better than that, of course, all the smartest people in the world had written books which were just sitting there. It was an ideas and information factory. So if you had the time, and could read everything in the library, Johnny figured that would probably make you *the* smartest person in the world.

Not that he had the time to 'download' all those books into his brain. He needed precise answers, as quickly as possible, to work out what could be done for his Mum and Dad.

He used the computer to research some of the things that had been happening at home, like the silence and the crying, and then he figured he would be best to pick up a real book, written by a real expert. And he was right.

It soon became obvious that the term 'being worried sick' wasn't just a saying at all. Worry, the type that had the Harrisons tightly in its grip, was (and is) a serious health hazard. The outcomes real and severe.

The stark realisation of what was happening to his family hit instantly. Johnny panicked, his heart fluttering and the chill ripping at him. But almost instantly he heard his mother's voice "Keep your heart burning bright darling boy, keep your heart burning bright." He caught himself, feeling self-conscious that his personal shockwave might have somehow unsettled the people sauntering around the library, such was its intensity. But the large room remained an oasis of calm (with the occasional outbreak of muffled politeness) as Johnny pressed on.

The research unearthed a couple of books that seemed seriously important, so Johnny decided he'd best take them home to study further.

But as he pedalled back home, and came around the corner into Blue Collar Crescent, his heart sank. It was perhaps the most awful sight he'd ever seen and the most horrible feeling he'd ever felt.

Out of nowhere it was as though he was smashed head-on by a ghost train – the recoil almost knocked him down, and each passing carriage impacted through him with a rhythmic, sickening shudder.

There was an ambulance with its lights flashing outside his home, and there was his Dad on a stretcher with a breathing mask, being put into the back. Everything was in slow motion – all images and no noise. Pure horror and fear. The icy claw had its massive clammy fingers all over him this time.

His mum was standing nearby, crying and shaking, and as he pedalled the Red Rocket as fast as it could go, there came another blow. His mother fell down and fainted, all seemingly in slow motion and silence, despite his efforts to reach her, and they put her into the ambulance too.

Strangers stood in the street watching, and some neighbours came up to Johnny and said some words. But they sounded like distant echoes.

In fact, the next few hours were a blur, a swirl, that Johnny would only ever remember in bits and pieces. An image here, some words there.

His Dad had to stay in the hospital. They said his blood pressure had gone way up. There were concerns he'd had a stroke, which being a brain injury, they explained, can affect whether you ever walk or talk properly again. If you survive.

And Johnny's Mum had collapsed from the shock. They were keeping her in the hospital too, under observation.

Mrs Howson from next door had taken Johnny to the hospital. Doctor Sally Stitchit had a long conversation with Mrs Howson, while Johnny sat in the corner. They both looked down towards the floor and stood with their heads close together, talking in whispers, occasionally glancing back at Johnny who was now still and numb. A dull, throbbing numbness, with the occasional image or snippet of conversation floating through his mind.

Eventually Mrs Howson took Johnny home. She said in her perkiest voice, "Well, I'd say it's best for you to sleep in your own bed tonight young lad. I'll sleep on the sofa and help you to get ready for school in the morning."

She kissed him on the forehead and then sounded much quieter: "Do try to get some sleep Johnny. Worrying about it won't make anyone better."

But with that, she closed the door to his bedroom.

And Johnny was alone.

Chapter 4

The Magician Materialises

All these years later, no one can remember for sure how or when he arrived on the scene – or where exactly he came from. But he certainly didn't drift into the picture either. It was more like he materialised on the stage. Alistair Farquhar seems to remember seeing him at the family home, at Grimsby Heights, back around the time the local factory shut down.

His name was Juan Kerr and he was a very curious character indeed.

There was some suggestion he had a connection with the *'Expanding Our Horizons – Making Life Cheap'* campaign, and he was a self-professed marketing genius. In fact, he was so good at marketing he even made up a fancy title for himself that other people could rarely get right, let alone understand.

Before too long he had convinced Alistair's father – The Third – that he should be paid a large amount of money, to make the Farquhars even richer than they already were.

He wore bright shirts, flicked both his hands in the air when he wanted to make a point, and spoke with a strange exotic accent that no-one could really pin down. The depth of his tan and the whiteness of his teeth seemed to defy Mother Nature, while his hair was somehow shaggy and perfectly in place, all at the same time. But he had charts, lots of charts – all colours and graphs.

One chart proved that he knew exactly what left-handed people wanted, while the other chart took care of the right-handers. At least, that's what his charts said.

Alistair (The Fourth) remembered thinking at the time that Juan's real skill was to confuse and convince people, in equal measure. The Third wasn't really too sure to start with, but he knew he liked money, and this new fellow seemed pretty sure of himself.

"There are many Juans and there are many Kerrs," the marketer declared in his strange accent. "Some have been so cruel as to describe them as *common*. But I am determined to be the greatest Juan Kerr the world has ever seen!" And that clinched it.

He was now working for *The Bat & Ball Company*, and things started to change pretty quickly.

The first thing he convinced The Third to do was to buy up any other companies that made bats and balls. It seemed like a strange notion, given everyone was getting along fine and making a perfectly good living. But Juan described them as competitors, who needed to be beaten. And the best way to beat them was to buy them and shut them down. So buy them they did.

Back when Horrie Harrison was in charge of Quality Control, the aim was to make products that people could trust. Products that were better than anyone else's. But now there were no more "anyone else's", because *The Bat & Ball Company* had shut them down. It was the only place that made bats and balls anymore, and

Juan had a cunning plan to sell more products than ever before – and he had the charts to prove it.

Juan also had a clever marketing term for it, that no-one could quite remember how to say, but it basically involved making things that would wear out. In fact, the company adopted a new slogan that appeared as a shiny gold sticker on all its products: *"Fun Before Fail"*.

What it meant was that, if you bought a bat or ball from now on, they would need to be replaced after a certain number of turns. You paid more for a product that would last longer, but the bats would eventually crack and the balls would deflate once they had been kicked or whacked for the set amount of kicks or whacks.

The top of the range bat had its own slogan "Crack A Ton Before It Cracks", while the cheaper models simply said "Belt It Before It Breaks".

The footballs, meantime, appeared in advertisements with the lofty promise of "75 Kicks of Quality".

From now on, anyone who loved to play games with bats and balls would have to keep buying new ones, to replace those that had worn out.

The business magazines described it as a 'brilliant strategy', which made Juan feel exceedingly right, and able to convince The Third to make even more changes.

The Bat & Ball Company had been selling bats and balls for a century, ever since Alistair Farquhar *The First* had whittled a piece of willow into a bat and won the inaugural championship for Grimsby United. Everyone asked him for a bat just like the one he'd used to hit the winning score.

Word spread, and before you knew it he had a busy factory churning out bats and balls for the entire country.

Now, 100 years later, The Bat & Ball Company was raking in the money – because people had to keep buying new bats and balls just to keep playing. It was around this time that Juan convinced The Third on an entirely new direction for the company, and used one of his favourite words (which sounded something like para-dime) to show he really knew what he was talking about. And his charts certainly left no one in any doubt. The Bat & The Ball Company was getting a new name.

It was going to be known as *The Box & All Company* – because they were now going to be making computer games.

Juan had been asking lots of people lots of questions. This research meant *The Box & All Company* knew exactly what people wanted (or, at least, what they thought of the questions they'd been asked). And it seemed just about certain that what people wanted was *The E-THRILLA 3000.*

The E-THRILLA 3000 was an emerald green box with hand-held controllers. It had three-thousand different computer games on it, but they were always being changed. If you wanted to keep up with the latest versions, you needed to buy the upgrades separately.

To try to make the locals feel better about the old factory shutting down, the new machine made its worldwide debut in Grimsby, complete with a free sausage sizzle and a special "Hometown Launch Thrilla Price!" of 3% off.

(Looking back now, with the benefit of hindsight, people said right from the outset it sounded different to other computer games. It had a drone-like hum, the screen would flicker wildly when it was starting up and, after a while, it had a fumy 'hot smell' to it. It was almost hypnotic to play.)

There were games where you pretended to play sport, and games where you could race cars, but mostly there were games where you tried to shoot more things than the other players.

It arrived with a big advertising campaign, showing famous people playing the games and having a great time. They'd say things like, "If you'd like your life to be as fantastic as mine, sit down and switch on to the E-THRILLA 3000."

But the true masterstroke was when Juan saw that the fashion darling of the entire world, Princess Blingalott, was holding her annual trends pronouncement. It was known as the *'U2-can-B-like-Me Decree'*. (No one ever explained why it was so clever to say it that way, but the world certainly stopped to listen.)

The Princess was the descendant of a famous European dynasty, but they no longer had their palaces to live in due to an uprising (and some bad arranged marriages in the 1700s). Instead, Princess Blingalott was the poster girl for all the leading fashion designers, perfume makers, and anything else that trendy people liked to buy. If she declared that poodles were the new accessory, then millions rushed out to buy poodles. One year she decreed that a limp was *individual and mysterious darlink*', so anybody who was anybody walked with a limp for the next 12 months.

Everyone waited on her trends pronouncement (it was much bigger than just an announcement) with breathless anticipation, and it was beamed live around the world.

Her decrees usually involved her main sponsors. Although no-one liked to say it that way. Instead, she was a 'Royal Ambassador' for the world's most expensive things.

Juan knew someone, who knew someone, who had a ticket to the pronouncement. He got them to take the new E-THRILLA 3000 to the after party, where everyone kissed each other's cheeks and behaved just like best friends. There were lots of photographers floating around and Princess Blingalott would swoon through the crowd for a few minutes, pretending to be incredibly interested in whoever she spoke to.

Juan's special agent (who happened to get a free holiday from The Box & All Company) moved into the royal vicinity and stuck out a hand to say hello. And of course, being polite, the Princess enquired as to what was that in the box. With photographers swarming around like flies the cameras flashed away wildly, sending pictures of Princess Blingalott and the E-THRILLA 3000 around the world.

Sales went through the roof and the business magazines went crazy. Their headlines trumpeted things like "A Right Royal Thrilla", "Juan Won To Be Number One", and "Princess Profit Power Play".

People soon started sleeping outside the stores, just to make sure they were first in line to buy an E-THRILLA 3000. And they would come back every week afterwards, to get the very latest upgrades.

Juan organised special sealed-off areas in the shops that people had to pay to go in to, to get their games and upgrades. Everyone seemed strangely happy and privileged about entering the *Thrilla Zones*, and felt especially clever as they dropped their coins into the turnstile and passed the sign declaring 'Admittance a Pittance'.

The Box & All Company was all set for the future – but the future was going to take a very unusual turn.

Chapter 5

Flowerpot Power

What ultimately made Ophelia Payne such a great reporter is that she really understood who was making the story, and who was doing the reporting. It can be a fine line, but she always understood where the line was. And in the media, this is not always the case.

Certainly she now had the powerful spotlight of the Grimbsy Gazette at her disposal and, yes, she did have ambitions to get ahead in her career. But her career and her own image were not the motivation for writing a good story. At the heart of it, she wanted to write about interesting and important things, and hopefully bring some justice to wherever it was needed.

She had to be careful though, because

journalists are a very queer bunch. The best ones have a vulnerable, human bit to them, but they have to wrap it up in armour so their workmates don't think they're weak and unreliable, especially when they have to go and report on truly horrible things.

For Ophelia, her reputation for telling it straight was something she rightfully took great pride in. Long after her colleagues had gone home or gone to the pub (or generally gone home from the pub), she could still be spotted in the far corner of the dark and empty Grimsby Gazette offices, a beacon of light pouring onto her notes from a small desk-lamp, and the keyboard clattering to the rhythm of her thoughts.

But by the time she got to work on the local paper, the boom times were long gone and just The Bat & Ball Company remained to pump black smoke into the sky, providing Grimsby with a still-beating pulse.

She marvelled that Grimsby and its people somehow kept surviving. Like a barnacle stuck on an ancient piece of wood that used to belong to a boat. If you grew up there, you couldn't wait to escape the place – in fact your whole being felt compelled to reject it – and yet, years later you'd come back full of warm feelings and great memories.

For the most part she loved the spirit of the people. Working hard, facing challenges, but with a respect for each other and the importance of community. And she especially loved the characters that still hung about the place.

They were wonderful fodder for her profile stories.

There was Andre 'The Angle' Andropov, the town's champion 400 metre runner whose left leg was decidedly shorter than the right. He was an ace running anti-clockwise, as he would automatically lean through the bends. But when they went the other way, he was in for a very long day.

There was Grimsby's most popular butchery, Mike's Mystery Meats. It had a sign in the front window that said "Savour The Secret – Because You Don't Know What We Put In Our Rissoles". Ophelia thought about blowing the story wide open by having laboratory tests done on the mystery meats, but then realised that sometimes unsolved mysteries are far better stories than dull scientifically proven facts. So she was smart enough to write a speculative piece, where she got locals to nominate what they *suspected* was sprucing up their sausages.

There was Stan 'The Statue' Sykes who could always be found leaning against the Town Hall. You couldn't tell whether the building was holding him up, or he was holding it up. They both seemed pretty set in their ways. Stan would look up and nod, and maybe even say your name. This was particularly unnerving when you'd been away on a long holiday and he'd just nod as though you'd passed him by moments before.

Grimsby's attempts at creating tourism jobs (once most of the factories had closed), were also rich pickings for Ophelia's reports.

One such exclusive centred on an organisation called the *Development and Advancement of Fiscal Tourism*, otherwise known as DAFT. Bringing in consultants – DAFT decided Grimsby needed a tourist attraction to make everything right. The old ball bearing factory was called upon for one final job, making two massive spheres to sit on the main road near the entrance to town. They were meant to represent the old world and the new, but they quickly became known as Grimsby's Big Balls. The media had a field day. (The committee later had the balls melted down to make 30,000 marbles – but the press still said they were nuts.)

Further attempts to gain attention also backfired, making Grimsby a laughing stock. They tried the idea of a Town Crier (who actually cried reading out the newspaper headlines). Then they tried to be even more 'creative' with the Town Liar, who would say three things and you had to pick the truthful statement. And finally, in pure desperation, they attempted to lure tourists with the Town Fryer, who introduced the world to the taste sensation known as the 'Grimsby Gagger'. It was an entire roast meal, about the size of a baseball mitt, encased in batter, and stuck on a handle. Health authorities were mortified, and even though many fast food corporations sent people in to investigate, the Gagger was soon banned under the Obesity Act, effectively choking off any last hopes of a tourism revival in Grimsby.

The council finally decided that DAFT was mad, and they were kicked out of their plush offices in the main street (which, in Grimsby, was called Grey Street). And as you headed along Grey Street, past the Town Hall, and past Stan 'The Statue' Sykes, you turned right into Ink Street, where the Grimsby Gazette was located.

The newspaper offices were in a restored old-style building, and proudly announced 'The Grimsby Gazette – You *Can* Handle The Truth'.

It was here, with Ophelia alone at her desk one night, that the call came in.

The call that would change the whole world.

"Ophelia, I have information," the caller said in a muffled, whispering voice that made it hard to tell if they were male or female.

"Who is this?" the reporter asked, even though Ophelia had a hunch. Her sixth sense (her news sense), had her pulse rising, her pupils sharpening, her pencil poised.

"My identity is not important, and must be kept confidential. But I need to share information with you that will be the biggest story of the year – and possibly of your lifetime."

The caller now certainly had Ophelia's attention, but refused to divulge their information over the phone, for fear of the conversation being bugged. (As fate would have it, the information would be in safe hands. For despite rampant speculation in the years that followed, Ophelia would never reveal the identity of her raspy-throated informant.)

It was arranged that a red ribbon would be placed around a flowerpot on a designated apartment window – one Ophelia walked past every day on her way to work.

"When you see that signal, meet me in the car park of the Grimsby Grand at 2am the following morning," the caller instructed.

"Come alone, don't be late, and be ready to take notes.

"Lots of them."

Chapter 6

Back and Beyond

Sometimes a strange thing happens when you lose something. You quickly realise just how much you *still have left*. And you learn to be grateful for what remains.

And that's why we now need to get back to Johnny, Horrie and Jenny Harrison – because a lot has happened, and a lot of time has passed, since the day the ambulance came.

So much time, in fact, that the government had somehow managed to hang on and get itself re-elected. Even though a growing number of people thought the *'Expanding Our Horizons – Making Life Cheap'* campaign had seen too many good things disappear *over* the horizon, never to be seen again. The mood was certainly changing.

But for now we must rewind. Back to Blue Collar Crescent, and back to where we left off.

Mrs Howson took care of Johnny for almost a week before his Mum came back. Jenny Harrison cuddled her son often and said she didn't know how, but they'd get through this together. And she was right.

Horrie, meantime, was alive, but he wasn't right.

He was going to have to learn how to walk and talk all over again. At first it was quite scary when Johnny went to visit his Dad. Horrie looked so crumpled up and could only say a few words, like "shovels", in a sad, crying sort of voice.

Strangely though, despite the shock of it all, there was the hint of a distant spark. Whether it was already within them, or came wrapped up with hope and a sense of forward momentum, the fact that they were still there together and the next day could be better than the last one, made Johnny feel the future wasn't as bleak as before.

Regardless of what was waiting for them on the horizon, even if it was still just out of view, there was a love and a bond that was going to shield them through.

And so began a painfully slow period of getting better for Horrie. He might never be like he was before, but he was going to get a bit better every day – and that was a good thing to know and to appreciate. They began to find positives in a situation that, in many ways, was tougher than anything they had known before.

One development even felt like pure luck. Their family GP, Sally Stitchit, referred Horrie to the world-famous medical specialist and inventor Sir Rennie Tee. (He'd once given her lectures at medical school.)

Sir Rennie specialised in helping people who'd had strokes and had invented the Nerve Ending Energiser, the Lame Leg Stimulator, and the Slack Jaw Massager. All these amazing devices helped people's bodies to remember what to do.

Sir Rennie was a roly-poly looking chap, with rosy red cheeks, and a fair bit of fun about him. "Rennie's the name Old Boy, but you can call me Sir for short!" he snorted, and sent Horrie off to exercise classes with the special machines. He also had the habit of yelling out "Hurrah!" when people were making progress.

Horrie eventually started being able to walk around using a cane and also put together more and more words. After a while, Horrie got his own cheekiness back. Sentences were a slow, deliberate grind, but he got to the point of saying strange things to the nurses like "If you … treat me right … today … I'll let … you … see … me cyst!" And everyone thought that was quite funny for some reason, even though Horrie didn't actually have a cyst.

As Horrie would later describe the situation, "it weren't all beer and skittles lad". His recovery took a very, very long time. And getting better can cost money, because you need to pay expert people to give you the best advice and exercises. Money, though, was something the Harrisons were fast running out of.

Horrie had been given a leaving payment from the factory, as part of the government's trade deal, and was also getting a small disability pension (which he was determined to cancel, just as soon as he was right). But with Horrie not working, and Jenny Harrison with only a few cleaning jobs left – plus all the medical bills coming in – it was like their money was the sand rushing through an old-style egg timer, disappearing faster and faster as it empties away.

Despite the daunting, almost impossible challenge of it all, Johnny never forgot the mission he'd set himself, and the importance of keeping hope burning bright.

He'd also formed a strong belief that the library held the key. Someone had even called it the 3D Internet. Because it wasn't floating around in space, waiting to be found (or missed). It was actually right there where you could see it. You could grasp the answers, pick them up, and take them home inside their books. It was real.

So every day after school he would pedal to the library and study what was on the shelves. In some ways, it was like his own adventure mystery, trying to crack the case. But with his Dad now getting good care, the focus had shifted to the financial health of his family.

In particular, he was exploring the business section of the library and ways he might be able to make some money. He'd already picked up some work delivering newspapers on his bike (and even though she said he should keep it, Johnny insisted his Mum use the money for the groceries). But he had far bigger plans than that – even though he hadn't quite worked out the exact details yet.

Apart from the business books, Johnny also took a keen interest in the biography section where he could find out about successful people (and how they did it). And he was also drawn to books about positive thinking, because it seemed to Johnny that good business needed good thinking to really succeed. And he was right.

He read book after book and started to understand the ways successful people had done things, even if he didn't quite know how he could make that happen in a place like Grimsby.

But a few stray ideas started to float around in his mind.

One day, after the regular paper run, Johnny had a final special magazine delivery for Clarrie Keeper, who ran the local antique shop. He wore a red and black chequered flannel shirt, had sandy coloured hair, a rock solid handshake, and a face that was as strong as granite, but still kind and open.

Clarrie was a long-time family friend

and was once the Mayor of Grimsby, back before Johnny was born. In fact, as a young alderman it had been his idea to hold the free dances in the town square, when all the old factories were operating.

Clarrie was one of those people who seemed to know everyone, and he certainly knew the Harrisons. It all started back when Horrie would buy excellent second-hand furniture off Clarrie for a great price.

"It's a sad business, that about your Dad – but you're a good lad Johnno, a good lad. I know you'll look after him and take care of your Mum too."

Clarrie's shop was full of stuff, mostly old stuff, and it was rather dark inside the shed, so it looked even older. It had a certain 'antique' smell. It wasn't a bad smell – just *distinct*. On the roof a sign was painted "Keeper Antiques – Good' uns At A Great Price".

Johnny asked Clarrie if he knew of any extra work going on the weekends, or during the holidays. (Apart from the regular paper run, Johnny occasionally earned some money doing odd jobs for people on the weekends – such as mowing lawns and washing cars – and he was always looking for an opportunity.)

Clarrie shook his head and said that since the factory shut down, there'd been no decent money flowing through the town to help the other businesses. So it was slim pickings all round. Then he paused and got Johnny to tell him about the books Clarrie had seen him riding past with most days.

Johnny was concerned he might sound a bit silly, especially if he didn't properly understand everything he'd been reading, but he spoke about what had interested him the most.

When he had finished talking, Clarrie paused again, then gave a curious glance and said "No extra work doesn't mean no opportunity lad, for all great ventures start out as ideas – nothing more, nothing less. Same with chairs and same with skyscrapers. And an idea can be as small as a laser beam or as big as the Moon, maybe even bigger."

Johnny wasn't totally sure what Clarrie was on about, but the former mayor of Grimsby took him through to the back room – where all the 'new' antiques were processed before going into the selling room. It was a stunning sight.

Piled up to the rooftop, in crates and buckets and bags, were thousands upon thousands *upon thousands* of bats and balls from The Bat & Ball Company. Not the new ones, in the fancy colours, but the old Grimsby ones – the ones that were made to last.

Clarrie picked up a bat, looked at the handle, and passed it to Johnny. There was a stamp on it "Tested and Approved – HH". Of course, HH were his Dad's initials and Johnny instantly got a lump in his throat just seeing it. This bat had been tested (possibly during the Quality Control Cup at lunchtime) and approved for sale in the shops.

But Johnny was stunned. How could people just abandon their beloved bats and balls? Was it because they were moving away?

"No lad, they're all still here." Clarrie explained. "But they've got nowhere to go and they've disappeared off the streets.

"See there's this here clever cove working for the company. He's realised he can't afford to have people holding on to bats and balls that will last a lifetime –

otherwise he can't get them started with his temporary ones.

"So he's done offered a swap deal – free cash – but only if you spend it on the new generation of bats and balls, or you can use the money to buy his brand new computer game. It's a devilishly clever plan, and most everyone has jumped at it."

It was true. In fact, there was a catchy advertising campaign just starting up for the exchange program called 'Why Work Out, When You Can Play In'.

Clarrie added: "And with no work around, people are switching off from the outside and plonking themselves on the inside to play this new computer game – because it's the most painless way for them to evaporate a day."

Clarrie then explained how the stores had absolutely no use for the old-style bats and balls, and had given truckloads to him for free – to save themselves a big dumping fee at the local tip.

They both sat there for a bit, lost in their own thoughts and memories, but Johnny sensed there was something missing. It was as if there was some reason why Clarrie wanted him to see the stockpile out the back.

As they walked through the dark shed, back towards the light coming from the front door, Clarrie said something curious.

"They were free to me, and they're free to you lad, if you can find them a purpose. And I do still have some connections at the council ..."

And with that he gave Johnny a wink, quick grin and little twist of the head that reminded him of his Dad. But there was something else to it as well.

Somewhere in there was an idea. Maybe it was Clarrie's or maybe one that Johnny needed to complete.

But there was certainly a promise of something big, floating around and just waiting to be caught and created. Polished and pitched. Waiting to be brought to life and ready to catch on.

Johnny thanked Clarrie, scooped up his library books, then jumped on the Red Rocket and headed for home. He didn't have the answers yet, but for the first time in a long time, he was full of energy and a sense of hope.

Chapter 7

The Decline and The Rise of The SLAKARS

The months clicked by like a stone stuck in a bike tyre, and the E-THRILLA 3000 was a hit. A massive hit. Across Grimsby and around the world.

Whereas people used to play games in the streets and the parks, with their bats and balls, most now stayed inside. You could only tell people were at home from the flicker of light coming off their screens and through the windows. That, and the occasional sound of shooting from the games they were playing.

But it's also important to say 'most' played games inside. Because a very important group of people – those so poor they couldn't afford the E-THRILLA 3000 (or even the extra electricity to power it) – were drifting about the place. Many of them still had their original Grimsby bats and balls, but weren't really playing old-style games anymore because it was hard to get enough people together for a proper go.

They just bumped into each other from time to time and had a polite chat, wandered around aimlessly, and eventually went home. Until that also became just too boring and they went out for another random ramble, hoping to bump into someone else they used to know. Little did they realise the part they would soon play in the dramatic events ahead.

And that's why we need to concentrate on the E-THRILLA 3000. Everyone (with any money to spare) had to have one. The newspapers screamed out headlines like "The Thrilla Gorilla" and ran competitions where you could win one, if you could provide 3000 reasons to stay inside playing computer games. They were swamped with entries.

It should be pointed out that all the newspapers were enthusiastic – bar one. For, much to the annoyance of Juan, the Grimsby Gazette continued to run stories

– quoting 'exclusive sources', which suggested there was some kind of safety concern about the new device. It seemed that special correspondent Ophelia Payne had access to inside information, but the story was yet to be fully revealed.

It didn't seem to bother The Third though. He was so impressed with how well things were going, that he decided to take his secretary on a working holiday to inspect the Fahraysha factory. All of the charts showed the company was going gangbusters, so The Third was happy to put Juan Kerr in charge while he was away. In fact, he gave Juan a promotion and allowed him to use even more words to describe himself on his business card.

The Third was actually planning to retire before too long, and while he was thrilled with the money Juan Kerr was making – it was his son Alistair who would *officially* be head of the company, even if he didn't have to make the decisions.

All the same, The Third thought it best to start training Alistair in the ways of the business, so he was required to go to Board meetings with lots of people in suits.

The rest of us might consider these meetings boring, with all the fiddly details about running factories and paperwork, but Alistair found it fascinating. He loved the thought of making things people enjoy using, and here was how it got done. Right inside the engine room.

And what Alistair enjoyed in equal measure were his computerised school lessons. Because rather than just talk to teachers, he got to talk to the scientists who had made the inventions, the sports-people who had broken the world records, the authors who had written the original books, and the adventurers who had made the discoveries, to name but a few.

The board meetings and his lessons were the highlights of his day, as life back in the compound got deadly dull once he'd finished a few laps of the swimming pool. For his father didn't like him venturing outside, just in case people were still angry about the factory.

But more time came and more time went, and Alistair continued to learn and grow, and to *change*.

In fact, the deadly dull time in the compound became something else – and something he actually started to look forward to. Solitude.

For after the excitement of his computer classes with the scientists and writers, and business leaders and Nobel Prize winners, the silence also gave him time to reflect about how things were, and how they might be. Not just in terms of the business, but life in general.

This silence – pure and just for thinking – became a very cherished and important time for Alistair. And, as fate would have it, an important development for Grimsby and beyond.

Alistair's mother, if you've been wondering, was often away shopping and skiing in different countries (in between running high-level fundraisers for worthy causes), but would drop by regularly with her favourite butler Fabio. Alistair didn't ask too many personal questions, but his parents were rarely in the same place together at the same time. However, they were very polite to each other, and kind to him. And his mother made sure she was home for his birthday and *always* gave him a ridiculously wonderful present.

The truth is Alistair was exceedingly

well looked after, whether his parents were there or not. There were people to do the cleaning, people to do the cooking, and he had a clear schedule of meetings and lessons scattered across the week. This was his version of 'normal'.

It was around this time, with The Third away and Alistair going to Board meetings that the whispers first surfaced. Something about "adverse reactions" to the E-THRILLA 3000. But because there was nothing adverse about the sales figures, no-one was overly concerned to start with.

The whispers, however, rang true.

The E-THRILLA 3000 was doing something to people's brains. It wasn't like Horrie's stroke, because people just kept on happily playing. But it was definitely triggering a response, which would go on to affect their bodies and their lives in a most significant way.

The world's most popular computer game was causing a 'chemical cocktail' of a reaction, with serious implications for every person who had prolonged exposure to the device.

What made it worse was that you didn't

realise it was happening to you. Everything seemed normal – up until the moment the world around you was just slightly out of whack. And by then, it was far too late.

Most people said they just felt like the house was a bit different. The shelves they used to put things on, up high, were now out of reach. Their pants constantly needed hemming and their view of the world was becoming different. They were seeing bits of furniture, like the underneath of tables, that they'd never paid attention to before.

Eventually, it couldn't be ignored any longer. People started venturing out of their homes again, if only to go to the doctor, and the Grimsby Gazette caught wind of a major medical emergency.

People were getting shorter.

Well, not the main part of the people. If you only saw them from the waist up, they looked just like they used to. But their legs had started to shrink – and would keep contracting until they became fat little stumps, with shoes on the end of them.

Afterwards people would say it didn't seem so bad at all, because it was painless. They just gradually adjusted to being shorter and, because it was happening to plenty of others, and so slowly, they didn't feel weird at all. Plus, their upgraded E-THRILLA 3000 always ran an advertisement before the start of each game saying "It's OK, You Don't Need To Go Anywhere, Because the Future is Right Here in Front of You. Play on!" And that made them feel quite OK about it all.

The Grimsby Gazette wasn't nearly so relaxed about the situation. Up-and-coming reporter Ophelia Payne headlined her exclusive: "ONE SMALL STEP FOR MAN".

Pretty soon the rest of the media got hold of it and busloads of scientists descended on Grimsby to work out what was going on. The condition would soon appear in other parts of the world, but had 'broken out' in Grimsby.

And before long it was confirmed. This wasn't just a stray, random occurrence, this was a common mystery illness. So it needed a name.

The scientists had a series of committee meetings and finally declared that they were dealing with 'Short Leg and Keyboard Accelerated Retardation Syndrome' – or SLAKARS for short.

And that's what people who had the syndrome started to be known as – the SLAKARS.

Dr Stitchit couldn't quite believe that people didn't seem to care, let alone understand.

"Now I like ice cream," she'd tell her patients. "If I have a little bit I feel good. But if I eat a whole lot I feel bad. And if I keep eating even more than that, I can get very sick indeed. Do you understand?"

And her patients would nod as though it was all very important, then waddle straight back home to their games.

One group that was concerned, quite rightly, were the good, hard-working folk who'd been *born* into a taller world. The so-called Little People. They quickly launched a group called 'Dwarfs Opposing Elongated Rhetoric & Stigma', otherwise known as the *DOers*. (For what it was worth, most SLAKARS would eventually become shorter than Dwarfs, by having virtually no legs at all.) However, the media quickly latched on to the term SLAKARS. So, despite the best efforts of the DOers, it stuck fast.

Back in the Boardroom, the suits

were certainly worried. Alistair was quite alarmed by what he was hearing, especially now his father had extended his working holiday with his secretary. The whispers were disturbing – *"This could be the end of the company"* … *"We could all be out of a job"* … *"Have we broken any laws?"*

As the whispers escalated into a nervous murmur and threatened to become a full-blown rumble, Juan Kerr strode into the room with his chest stuck out and a big smirk on his face, along with several very impressive looking charts.

"My dear, dear colleagues," he said. "We have a wonderful opportunity before us!"

And then, as the stunned faces looked back at him he added:

"This may be the greatest thing to ever happen to this company."

Chapter 8
Owning The Game

SLAKAR Syndrome spread around the world rapidly. There were SLAKARS everywhere – not that they seemed to mind. But the newspapers and governments were outraged, and The Box & All Company was seen as the villain. If just for a fleeting moment.

Scientist after scientist published their findings, showing that only people using the E-THRILLA 3000 were experiencing painless leg shrinkage. Some scientists put forward theories about the toxic chemicals that were part of the device, while others claimed radiation, or even the flickering light from the screen was to blame. Each of them tried to draw attention to their own, individual findings. And that's where they all failed.

Because even though it seemed such an undeniable truth, the individual scientists didn't seemed to be agreeing with each other on exactly why it was happening. Certainly, not in a way that left everyone totally convinced. Each scientist had their own strong case, but the public wanted a universally accepted and easy-to-understand answer.

As it stood there was plenty of separate evidence and theories, and plenty of people with short legs, but the scientists hadn't collectively (or convincingly) delivered an iron-clad explanation. They just presented different pieces of the puzzle.

The evidence, as strong as it was from the scientific point of view, wasn't considered *official* or *complete* by the broader community. The strands had not been woven together into a single plausible story. So with so much different information flying around, the question (to the public's mind at least) was certainly not settled.

This allowed the wily Juan to work his own form of magic. He kept a close eye on everything that was being said until he heard what he wanted to hear – a scientist who didn't think the E-THRILLA 3000 was responsible.

His name was Sasha Schmell and he had been a champion debater at school. He always liked to take the most impossible side of the debate, because he loved turning people around to his point of view. (He knew he'd done particularly well if he'd managed to convince himself as well.)

He and Juan hit it off straight away, to the point where The Box & All Company was proud to 'privately' fund Schmell's next research project.

Juan knew it didn't matter if 1,000 scientists said the E-THRILLA made your legs shrink. Yes, the legs were definitely shrinking, but that mattered not. Because he could make just one scientist 1,000 times *more famous* than all the others, so that Sasha's voice was the only one people would hear and remember.

Sasha Schmell claimed shorter legs were a natural evolutionary cycle, which would all sort itself out in the next million years or so. So you really had nothing to worry about.

Juan sent him on a worldwide media

tour (staying at the very best hotels and visiting all the sights along the way). Sasha went on TV shows and news bulletins to let everyone know that the other scientists obviously couldn't agree and therefore didn't really know what they were talking about. So you should happily keep playing the E-THRILLA 3000. And that's exactly what people did.

Only the Grimsby Gazette and reporter Ophelia Payne refused to play along, wheeling out exclusive after exclusive and 'informed sources', which countered Schmell's claims and seemed to be very informed indeed.

However, The Box & All Company didn't stop with Sasha Schmell alone. Not by a long shot.

It had what Juan Kerr described as his favourite "LOLs". Lawyers On Lobbyists.

The lobbyists got paid to make sure the rule-makers in the government made laws that suited their cause. Or, in this case, The Box & All Company. They pretended to be best friends with the politicians and took them to lunch, and got them (and their families) into the best concerts and sporting events. And they made sure the politicians saw what 'prominent' scientist Sasha Schmell had to say about the E-THRILLA 3000 and how other scientists couldn't completely agree on anything for certain.

And, before long, the politicians started to nod their heads and the lobbyists didn't need to say much more at that point.

The lawyers, meantime, threatened to take anyone to court – and sue them for a lot of money – if they made claims that they couldn't prove about The Box & All Company.

And because the lobbyists had convinced the politicians to bring in the new 'Slakars Act' (where you couldn't say anything bad about the E-THRILLA 3000, because that might cause possible embarrassment and unfounded mental hurt to its users), sales figures continued to rise.

Now Juan could really get moving. With SLAKARS unable (or unwilling) to leave their couches, and the law on his side, The Box & All Company embarked on a series of campaigns with so-called partner organisations – allowing them to make even more money.

One promotion was with Pizza Corp

called "Power Up To Play". It involved people ordering food online, through their E-THRILLA 3000s, and having their meals delivered directly to their couches. There were all sorts of pizzas available, including the 'Health Stacker' (3 pizzas with *low fat* cheese, for the same price as two regular pizzas).

A competition with The Travel Bug company put a call out for the best limbo pictures. Perfect for SLAKARS, and the competition even made fun of long-legged people. It noted 'gawky Ganglies' need not apply, and a lot of SLAKARS had fun about that one on the 'Thrilla Family' web forums, adding comments like "let's face it, they're too poor to play anyway."

The limbo competition worked well because you could use the E-THRILLA's inbuilt camera to take the limbo picture, in between games. You could win a world trip, or a whole year's worth of game upgrades. The winner took the upgrades.

But it wasn't all about promotions and competitions. For while the critics had been silenced, the suits at The Box & All Company were still nervous about whether their computer game might cause even more problems down the track – or, worse still, if the negative scientists started employing their own lobbyists to change the rules (but they never did).

Juan, however, made them all feel pretty clever when he appeared with the head of the Health Department to announce *The Box & All Wellness Foundation.*

The company would provide medical equipment for the children's wards of leading hospitals around the world, and the kids there would be allowed to play the E-THRILLA 3000 for free. The company won all sorts of awards for being a great 'corporate citizen'.

In return, the government gave The Box & All Company a special tax deal which allowed it to set up its own 'research and development program'.

The 'extraordinary opportunity' to join this new research and development program was promoted exclusively through the Thrilla Family web forums. It meant that a select few would be allowed to test out the very newest games before anyone else! 6,397,521 people applied, even though it meant the 100 successful applicants would need to re-locate to Grimsby

HQ (which was a fancy way of describing a specially prepared room in the old, empty factory).

Relocating didn't seem to bother anyone at all, because The Box & All Company would also give the winners little portable scooters, that they could park next to their couches and drive all the way up the special ramps at Grimsby HQ.

And what a sight awaited them.

No one seemed to mind that the stools they would sit on – all in neat long rows – meant their feet wouldn't touch the ground all day. It didn't matter, because they weren't planning on going anywhere else.

There, in front of the lucky 100, were the shiniest, biggest computer screens, with amazing new games waiting to be played. And the pizza went past on a conveyor belt (including the low-fat cheese option for the health conscious).

Juan stood beaming before the winners and they sat, with their little legs paddling, beaming right back at him.

And a great cheer went up when he said, "Comrades, you are the true winners!"

"You will help us to make the next

generation of games, that the rest of the world gets to love."

And then he paused, and sounded serious "except for those poor Ganglies out in the street who don't know any better." And a couple of SLAKARS down the back had a bit of a cough-laugh under their breath. Although most nodded along with Juan and pretended to care about the poor Ganglies.

"But we will do what we can for them in good time," he added quickly.

"For now, enjoy your time here as the most fortunate people in the world!"

As he said that, he clapped his hands together twice, the lights dimmed right down and the screens came to life. It was extraordinary.

There were completely updated versions of *Bloodbath Bounty*, right through to entirely new games, such as *Hunt For The Long-Legged Zombies*.

Many in the room that day said it was the most beautiful thing they had ever seen.

Chapter 9

The Man and The Plan

Clarrie Keeper wasn't just a good man, he was a clever man. A *very* clever man. The former mayor of Grimsby had been a long time 'semi-retired' at his antiques shop, but he was the sort of person who had the rare ability to instantly reconnect with people he hadn't seen for years and years.

He also knew that – despite what the loudest SLAKARS were saying about Ganglies – there were still plenty of people who didn't fancy the idea of their legs shrinking, no matter how painless it might be. And he knew that the government was also very worried about going broke if people kept changing size.

Because if everyone got shorter, no-one would be able to reach the handstraps on the buses, get their bags into the overhead lockers on the aeroplanes, or reach the coin slots on the vending machines. Let alone get to most of the supermarket shelves. So everything was rapidly becoming useless.

The economy was in a bad way and, to make matters worse for the government, there was yet another election looming. This time around, the rival *Vote 1 For Us Party* was getting a lot of support for its "Bringing Our Jobs Back Home" campaign.

Clarrie knew that an election campaign is a perfect time to get some action happening, because politicians like to convince people they have the answers. Clarrie also happened to know Henry Stamper, who was the top public servant in the land. They used to play on the same school football team, before Henry moved to the big city. As Chief Secretary to the Executive, it meant Henry worked for whoever was the government, to help them put their plans into action – and even gave them advice when needed (which was more often than you might imagine).

Even though Clarrie knew plenty of people from all walks of life, he always treated them the same – as people. Big or small, rich or poor. Because he figured he was a person too. And he was right.

Having been good friends with Horrie Harrison for many years, Clarrie could see the same spark in his son. That special something that connected with people. It could be encouraged, but not smothered. You needed to give the person enough air to grow – to get there themselves.

And so it was with Johnny, who started dropping by every day for a cup of tea out the back – amid the masses of classic old bats and balls. Clarrie would ask lots of questions about the books Johnny had been reading and what he'd learned, and they would even talk about how The Box & All Company had been so effective in getting people to change their habits.

Johnny looked forward to the visit each day, after doing his research at the library. He felt like his ideas were worth something when he spoke with Clarrie and that ideas could easily become real – if treated right.

Plus, Clarrie would tell a few stories about how things got done in the old days, and the ways rule-makers think – especially when they're trying to get elected. Just some handy suggestions that had the habit of sticking in Johnny's mind and joining-up with other ideas, until such time as he had a plan.

The plan had been forming as Johnny rode the Red Rocket around, delivering his papers for extra money to help out at home. The playing fields, that used to be full of games and laughter after school, were now mostly empty. There may be one or two bored people standing around, talking about not much, but the fields were depressingly quiet.

The SLAKARS, as we know, had been poking a lot of fun at Ganglies (mostly, Johnny thought, to feel better about themselves). But it was certainly true that the majority of people who didn't have an E-THRILLA 3000 simply couldn't afford one. Eventually some of these people started thinking about ways to get money in a hurry – which can be a dangerous thought to have. So there was now a sense of urgency about finding a way forward not only for Johnny's family, but for people far and wide.

One afternoon, Johnny felt brave enough to share his plan. He'd wanted to do it for some time, but was worried Clarrie might laugh at him or say he was wrong – which is a fear people with plans should always ignore. (Because, after all, "no" is such a small word, it's not worth being scared of.)

"Mr Keeper, I have an idea for making people healthy in their bodies and their minds and, well, I'm wondering if you might share it with your friends who are still on the council.

Clarrie just looked, still and polite, and kept listening intently, so Johnny went on.

"I think it's just what Grimsby needs right now – and maybe everywhere else too. I've even typed it up on the computer at the library and printed it out.

Johnny held the plan in his hand, and then said the extra bit he wanted to add – but wasn't sure if it sounded a bit selfish or desperate (but he said it anyway).

"Well, it could be a lot of work but I could help run it after my other jobs and I would really, really be grateful if my Dad could be involved. He's back home now and getting better, and this would be the best thing for him. Plus I know he'd really make it fun for everyone."

Clarrie didn't laugh. He just smiled in a positive way and said, "I'm sure your Dad would make it great, Johnno.

"Now explain to me how it works lad."

Chapter 10

Stamper Strikes

By the time Johnny had finished explaining his vision for the future, there was a long pause.

Clarrie Keeper gazed thoughtfully all the way from the back room, where they were sitting among the bats and the balls, to the light bursting through the front door of his antiques shop. Such a pause would normally have made Johnny nervous, but not this time.

"You're a good'un Johnno. Let me have a bit of a think."

Then Clarrie stopped gazing ahead, looked directly at Johnny and said: "And whatever you do, don't stop thinking like that – even if Plan A gets knocked down, there's always Plan B, and after that, *well,* there's plenty more letters in the alphabet.

"But I tell you what lad, can you let me keep that copy of your idea? – I'll give it back to you when I see you next."

Johnny was happy for Clarrie to take a closer look. It meant that his ideas had created interest. Some value to someone else. That his thoughts weren't silly after all.

But as he pedalled home, Johnny knew there were some weaknesses with his plan – like who would pay for it all. He'd hoped that by offering to run things, it might make the local council more interested, and give him the opportunity to earn a little more for the family. Mostly, though, he just wanted to see his Dad getting out and having a laugh.

As always, as he got closer to home, his thoughts turned to his parents – both still trying to be positive, especially around Johnny. They would make little jokes with each other as Horrie did his exercises, and slowly but surely he started to move much better and speak quite clearly.

In fact, every so often, he could walk for a little way without needing the help of his stick. He'd fill out his progress forms and send them off to the specialist Sir Rennie Tee, who would drop by once a month and they'd have a cup of tea with the 'Wedding China'. Sir Rennie would talk about anything and everything (except Horrie's health) which strangely made Horrie feel pretty good about himself. Just about normal in fact.

But the truth remained that, despite Johnny's invaluable help to slow the drain, the money was still running out, and who knows what would happen when it finally did.

For the next week or so, Johnny kept up his routine of school, odd jobs and library visits, although the Antiques Shop was closed as he pedalled past on the paper run. It had a sign on the front "Away Today – And Maybe Tomorrow".

Whenever he rode past he wondered if the shop's worldly owner had taken another look at his plan, and figured 'The Nice Negotiator' (as his newspaper adver-tisements described him) would probably do that when he got back.

But this wasn't the case at all, and the Harrison's world was about to change again. Dramatically.

Late on Friday afternoon came a knock at the door, and there was Clarrie Keeper in the company of a big man who was in a very neat, dark, pin-striped suit. The fellow had a round friendly face, with a reddish nose and an old-style big moustache which was twirled at the ends – and it has to be said that it suited him.

The pair was invited in and Mrs Harrison put the kettle on straight away while plenty of small chatter and banter went on in the modest little kitchen. Everything came to a crashing halt though, when it got round to introductions and Clarrie said: "Horrie, Jenny, Johnno – I'd like you to meet the Chief Secretary Henry Stamper. He's here to talk about Johnno's plan for the future."

It was like everyone had been hit by a stun-gun (especially as Horrie and Jenny didn't even know Johnny had been working on his plan).

After an awkward silence, Horrie yelped in a panic "Jenny, the Wedding China!" Then everyone laughed and Mr Stamper said it wasn't necessary at all, so the banter and chatter resumed instantly and continued on for ages. It was as if they'd known the Chief Secretary all their lives and almost forgot that they were in the midst of a highly peculiar situation.

After the cup of tea, Henry cleared his throat and said: "Now then, Clarrie came down to see me this week and brought me your plan Johnno, and the government is keen.

Then he whispered across to Clarrie (but everyone could hear it): "In fact, the lower the opinion polls go, the keener they get – and they're *very* keen indeed!" Clarrie and Henry both had a quick chuckle about that one.

But not Johnny, Horrie and Jenny. They were just sitting there, gobsmacked at what they were hearing. So Stamper, glancing around the table, pressed on.

"Right! You see – how can I put this – governments don't always have the best ideas, but they like to put forward the notion that they have. And right now, what with the SLAKARS crisis hurting the economy, and the election coming up, well, the government is keen to be doing something. *Anything really.*

"Your plan young man is tailor-made for the current situation, not just here in Grimsby, but across the entire country.

And, if it catches on, well, it could go even further. The government just needs to give it a name, something catchy you know, and roll it out as quickly as possible – before the election – as its own idea for a better future."

The Harrisons remained the same – looking like shop window dummies in a display – with Horrie holding a cup of tea, frozen, near his mouth.

Henry thought he must have missed something and then added:

"Oh, I'm so sorry. And of course we want you to run it Johnno. To be, you know, *'the face of the future'* and all that sort of thing. And we want your parents involved too, just like in your plan, *but much bigger*. And don't worry, we will organise things with your school so you don't miss out on your education.

Johnny, Horrie and Jenny remained as rigid as crash test dummies. Henry and Clarrie glanced at each other, wondering what to do next.

Then came a sentence that seemed to come out a bit slower than the others, and hung in the air for ages.

"And, of course, we will be paying you

all proper money to run the thing for us."

Silence. Stunned stillness. It was almost a noisy silence that got more and more noisy as it went on. Until at last Clarrie finally ventured. "Is, ah, that all right?"

Horrie, still frozen with his cup near his mouth, squeaked out all he could manage, staring off into space. "Fine."

With those words, the freeze shattered, everyone breathed out and the life came back into them and they looked around and shared a laugh, still not quite believing what had just happened to their lives. As the banter broke out again, and the detail got discussed, Jenny Harrison gave Johnny a look bursting with pride, and the young man felt the best he had for some time.

Then a massive smile broke out under Henry Stamper's moustache. He clapped his big hands together and boomed: "Tally-ho chaps! Let's get moving!"

Chapter 11

The Black and White Arrow

Juan always needed the arrow on his charts to be pointing upwards, day after day and week after week. Otherwise, it would affect his mood, and an angry Juan Kerr is not someone you want to be around.

What it meant was he couldn't be happy unless he was converting more and more people to the E-THRILLA 3000 (and creating more and more cases of SLAKAR Syndrome in the process).

The fact that the company was making more money than it had ever made before didn't matter. The arrow had to be pointing up. And if anything threatened the arrow, Juan needed to know why.

So you can imagine his horror when he read about the government's new national

LEADERS program (which was short for the Learning, Exercise And Development Revival Scheme). It was a scheme to get people and the economy moving again, and the government was pushing it hard (especially with the election getting closer).

The Grimsby Gazette even carried a photo of Johnny, next to Horrie in his umpiring outfit, and Jenny holding some team uniforms. *"Local Family Getting The Nation Back on Its Feet – One Game At A Time"* declared the story, by the award-winning journalist Ophelia Payne.

But it was the detail of the plan that worried Juan most, for things had been gradually changing ever since the old Grimsby factory closed down. Back then there were no extra jobs around. But since more and more people had become hooked on the E-THRILLA 3000, developing SLAKAR Syndrome and becoming couch-bound, things had swung the other way. Now there were jobs cropping up everywhere – but no one qualified to do them.

However, there was a pool of people keen to have those jobs. The ones left behind. The poorest of the poor who couldn't afford to buy into all the new bats and balls and computer games. They were the main targets for the LEADERS program.

The scheme involved schools, book companies, libraries and sporting organisations across the country. To be part of the LEADERS program you would be trained up not just for the job that interested you most, but you also took part in traditional outdoor games, and then one person each week nominated their favourite book and the author would turn up to speak to everyone. Whether it was a detective book or a cookbook, it didn't matter. And often it wasn't so much about the book, but being able to share your ideas without worrying what the other person might say. Ideas were encouraged, even if you had a different point of view.

The program also made sure everyone could swim, perform first aid, and speak well in front of others.

It was about being healthy, happy and getting a broad education. Not only was there a job at the end of it all, but the government even paid you to take part.

The book companies loved it, because it got people reading their books again. The sporting organisations loved it, because it got people playing their sports again. The schools loved it, because people actually enjoyed learning stuff they wanted to learn. And the people taking part loved it (even more than they imagined they might), because not only did they get paid, and have a future and hope, but they started mixing and meeting a whole range of new friends.

They felt alive again.

The LEADERS program also included plenty of free choices, which allowed you to study extra things that interested you, like forming a band or learning to paint. You could even get free access to the Internet and computer games (but the time was quite limited so that everyone got a turn and there was no risk of 'over exposure').

All of this didn't worry Juan so much. People that were too poor to buy his games didn't really appear on his charts to start with. But as he read the Grimsby Gazette further, and reached the last part of the story, a look of loathing and defiance swept across his face.

"The LEADERS program will also be adapted to those people with the condition known as SLAKAR Syndrome. Any person in this category will be provided with free computer upgrades, for the period of their involvement, on the strict condition that they take part in the OUT (Outside & Upright Transition) component."

The article concluded: "Extra upgrades will be provided to those who commit a *greater* amount of time to the OUT component, which will be tailored to their individual physical needs."

Juan's blood ran cold. As far as he was concerned, his arrow was under threat.

Now some may say this was an over-reaction. The LEADERS program wasn't banning anyone from having a choice. It was actually giving them more choices and it was giving SLAKARS the thing they craved – free gaming upgrades.

Cleverly, the government had avoided getting itself into trouble with the lobby-ist-created 'Slakars Act', because it made no direct mention of the E-THRILLA 3000. Thanks to this legal loophole, the government had not broken its own laws.

Had Juan been thinking more clearly, he would have immediately sent a message out on the 'Thrilla Family' web forums offering free upgrades of his own, to keep his people on the couch.

But at the end of the day, even his SLAKARS were running out of money. While they kept playing, the electricity bills and pizzas kept arriving – with monotonous regularity – and the power company and delivery people needed to get paid. Juan had long dreaded such a day. But then he had another brainwave.

If the poorest people were now getting paid to take part in the LEADERS program, they would suddenly have the money to afford the E-THRILLA 3000. So getting his SLAKARS to take part was not such a bad idea after all. He could use them to convince all the others about how great the device was, and sales would go through the roof yet again.

It seemed like a cunning and wonderful plan. One that the business magazines would applaud, and give out awards for. But it didn't work out that way.

To start with the SLAKARS rode their scooters down to the sporting field, generally in a horrible mood. They were keen to get it over and done with, and get back to their couches with their free upgrades and a LEADERS payment to help with the electricity and pizza bills. Then they could "switch on and switch off" as they described it.

But out there, in the fresh air and the sunlight, with no Long Legged Zombies to slaughter, with no Bloodbath Bounty to tally at the end of a three-day marathon, things were different. Very different.

So different, in fact, that they were real. With real people.

At first it seemed a bit scary to go up to a real person and start talking. But before you knew it, "I know you – what have you been up to?!" Most of the time the answer was an embarrassed "Not much" but then with a "Same here" the conversation would flow, based mostly around the things they used to do "on the outside".

Then, when they went home and started playing the E-THRILLA 3000 their thoughts would drift back to the highlight of their day. Not the day-high score they'd managed to rack up on Wizard's Gizzards, but getting to see Bill, or Harry or Sarah or Penny again. And not just that, but the running and the catching and the laughing and the razzing. It had just been something special.

Soon a lot of the SLAKARS started thinking about re-inventing themselves. They loved to play on their computer, and that was fine, but the whole day and every day just seemed to be a bit much really. It suddenly felt hollow to spend an entire day (or week) on the computer. Being out in the open, laughing, mixing, believing, and dreaming – and dreaming for real – was a whole different universe.

It used to be that SLAKARS felt quite clever playing their games, making fun of Ganglies, and sending e-notes to each other as they went along. Now their thoughts turned to what they really wanted to be. The choices were all there. Real and right in front of them.

In a lot of cases it wasn't about the job they used to have, for here was the chance to get trained and create the life you wanted most and had never known. Suddenly *life* was 'the big game', and totally exciting, and the E-THRILLA 3000 was something you could fit in at the end of the day, or even on the weekends. It was just *a* game. Not *the* game.

Juan's arrow was in trouble. He

monitored the chat groups. He knew what the tribe was thinking and feeling, and his great achievement was in trouble. He was trying not to be desperate, but he was getting nervous.

He eventually sent out a carefully worded survey to all E-THRILLA 3000 users, to ensure players continued to "have the greatest experience in the world".

When the answers came back he sliced and diced the data. He looked at the ages, the genders, at the backgrounds, and everything that made the SLAKARS tick. It seemed there was only one course of action to ensure the E-THRILLA 3000 remained the coolest of the cool.

It had to be jet black. (Well, jet black with some dark blue lights that glowed when you turned it on.)

The old emerald green box was gone. The media releases went out, with a full-blown advertising campaign. "It's The New You – Get Black & Blue". The factory in Fahraysha revamped the production line and the new generation game was being made in its millions. It even had a new name. The BLACK MAX 4000.

The process was costly and the factory

conversion took an extremely long time, but it was the company's money and Juan knew even bigger things were ahead. His charts said so.

Juan came up with a transfer plan that would allow people to trade in their old E-THRILLA 3000 for the new BLACK MAX 4000, by paying just a small fee. And to entice them, owning the new product was the only way to access the hottest, latest computer games – all 4,000 of them. They called it an exclusive offer (although it was exclusive to whoever could afford the transfer fee).

Juan felt pretty good. Despite all the dramas of the LEADERS program, he had found a way to re-invent the fortunes of The Box & All Company. He had done it again. And his arrow was definitely pointing up.

With word finally through that truck-loads, shiploads and planeloads of the BLACK MAX 4000 were about to be heading out of Fahraysha, to destinations around the world, he suddenly remembered. Tonight was the night.

Princess Blingalott's annual trends decree was being beamed live around the world.

He sat back in his chair, relaxed and content. As the TV came on, to herald the arrival of Princess Blingalott they released white doves.

Then the unicorns walked onto the stage, followed by the Polar Bears, and the Swan Lake ballerinas. Juan's eye started to twitch.

Finally the fake snow began falling and Princess Blingalott appeared in a white diamond chariot, pulled along by a stunning pale horse, and flanked by albino guardsmen. She was wearing a platinum blond wig.

Juan stood up. His skin crawling. A cold clammy sweat on his unnaturally tanned brow.

"Yes my darlinks, you are right. Zee future is Vite. Totally Vite!

"Vite, bright and upright!"

The crowd cheered.

Juan immediately went to his office, calmly packed up his charts, and was never seen in Grimsby again.

Chapter 12

The Phone Call

Time had certainly ticked on, and so much has been happening elsewhere that we need to get back to Alistair Farquhar the Fourth. Like Johnny, things had been moving quickly, and he had been growing up faster than most.

In fact, it's worth noting that they were rarely referred to as Alistair or Johnny anymore. Instead, it was Al (or sometimes *A4*) and Johnno. So best we do the same.

Certainly, they were no longer the boys of the old factory days. They were very much young men, with plenty on their plate and they were being noticed. (To the point where the *Tattler* gossip column in the Grimsby Gazette took an increasing interest in their respective romantic relationships, but that's a whole other story.)

When Juan suddenly left the company, Al was properly in charge – and feeling totally alone. He'd technically been the head of the company ever since The Third and his secretary decided to extend their overseas holiday into actual retirement. But because Juan had been the person who'd made so much money, Al had never really been making the decisions. Just signing the pieces of paper to approve Juan's ideas.

However, as we know, The Third had been making sure his son was trained up in the ways of business. And apart from watching Juan's certain kind of brilliance up close, A4 had been tutored by the very best business leaders from around the world, via computer hook-up. He'd had a lot of time to reflect on how to run a company, as well as the other stuff that really interested him – the big ideas in life. And now was his time.

The truth be known, Al had never warmed to Juan. He understood that the company was there to make money. But making as much money as it possibly could, to the damage of other businesses and people, always made him feel uncomfortable.

He saw business as something he later described as 'The Triple Treat'. A win for the company making the products, by creating a profit. A win for the workers, by giving them and their families a good income and a future. And a win for the customers by giving them something that worked as well as it promised (and hopefully even better). It was a very old-fashioned idea but, like Johnno, Al had studied business from the best.

When it all came down to it, A4 believed that good business was about having a genuine ongoing relationship with someone. And that's why now, alone in his big corner office, he was facing a crisis – one that was about to get a whole lot worse. Thanks to the annual Blingalott pronouncement, the world was going white. But The Box & All Company was black to the max.

Al knew he couldn't find the solution from the suits in the boardroom. They were nice enough people, but The Third had only put them there to say 'yes' whenever he needed someone to say 'yes' to one of his plans (or one of Juan's charts). Al didn't need a 'yes', he needed an answer.

But before he could even tackle that issue, the phone rang.

"Mr Farquhar, good morning, I am Professor Rhonda Rodriguez from the Stealth Institute, and I am calling about the payment for our research," the strange voice said.

Al was puzzled but quick to respond, firmly but politely: "Professor, I am afraid I don't know who you are, or anything about your research."

The professor paused and then said. "You may not know me, Mr Farquhar, but I am sure you know your former executive Mr Kerr."

There was now some doubt and curiosity in Al's voice: "Yes I do. But what about him?"

Professor Rodriguez then went on to explain that Juan Kerr had commissioned secret research, to determine whether the E-THRILLA 3000 could be *proven* to be the source of SLAKAR Syndrome (even though he was paying the world famous scientist Sasha Schmell to tell everyone it was perfectly fine).

The reports had come in, and it was the worst possible news.

The Stealth Institute had confirmed a link between prolonged use of the E-THRILLA 3000 and SLAKAR Syndrome. As strongly suspected, but not clearly established (in the public eye at least), the theories were correct.

A4 was sick to his stomach, feeling a thumping pain as if he'd been punched off-guard, and left fighting the urge to throw up.

The Syndrome was being caused by a *combination* of extended exposure to radiation, and the particular hypnotic frequency of light flicker from the E-THRILLA games. In addition, the fumy vapours given off by the components – once the machine started to run hot after two hours – created a chemical reaction in the brain that affected the glands and nervous system, triggering the accelerated shrinkage of the legs. Especially legs that remained inactive for many hours on end.

Al was in shock – his breathing shallow, his hands shaking, a cold sweat crawling over him. He looked out his window at the empty haunting skeleton of the old factory, and then he looked at the picture on his walls of all the happy workers playing for the Quality Control Cup, with the trucks piled full of bats and balls about to head off to the shops.

He caught his reflection in the glass of one of those pictures. Him. The newly installed head of a company that had changed the world. Finally here, in the place he'd always been destined for – running the great family enterprise – only to find it desolate, soulless, and facing immediate and ultimate doom.

Al couldn't help feeling cheated. He would be remembered as the person in charge when the mighty business crashed down, in shame. Even though it was the actions of others that had delivered this cruel moment.

It was a deep, sharp stabbing hurt – but almost immediately his thoughts turned to those poor wretched souls with 'Short Leg and Keyboard Accelerated Retardation Syndrome'. The SLAKARS.

They may have bandied together into some form of protective tribe, or gang, and almost sealed themselves off from the rest of the world – like a caterpillar in a cocoon

– but they were trapped all the same. Sure, they lived in a free world, but Al realised the limited choices they now had were not the choices they deserved, and were not completely of their making. His company had effectively herded them to where they now found themselves.

"Hello, Hello! ... Mr Farquhar – are you there?!"

Al snapped out of his shock, and back to the conversation on the phone. "Oh, yes, Professor, I'm sorry. It's just so much to take in. But tell me, is there anything – anything at all – that can be done to reverse the condition?"

Here at last was some small slither of hope. Not so much for A4 and his doomed company, but for the people with SLAKAR Syndrome.

Professor Rodriguez stressed that the chance of recovery was by no means conclusive, but it was felt the 'subjects' could *potentially* regain the elasticity within their legs and very gradually return to their normal height over a period of 12 to 18 months. However, this would involve a sustained program of physical exercise, and a definite limit on the use of the

E-THRILLA to no more than 90-minutes per day, to ensure the system didn't overheat, give off its fumes, and trigger the same reaction with the radiation and light flicker as before.

"So again, sir," the Professor emphasised, "We just don't know at this stage if people will *ever* be able to make a full recovery.

"I am happy to provide you with the reports – Mr Kerr had insisted they be kept confidential and for his eyes only – but, there is, of course, the matter of payment for the research."

Al Farquhar thanked the Professor and promptly arranged the payment, and for the secret reports to be sent directly to him (and nobody else) immediately.

He then contacted his assistant, who worked in a room outside his office, and requested four phone numbers. She appeared some moments later and put a piece of paper in front of him. He thanked her and sent her home for the day.

The first call was easy. He immediately phoned the scientist Sasha Schmell – the man who had been denying any link between the E-THRILLA and SLAKAR

Syndrome – and calmly cancelled his worldwide tour, along with the funding for his research project, and wished him all the best for his future.

Al put down the phone with a chilling dread about what to do next. It was a sickening mix of fear and the cold, hard truth.

He had just one more call to make, but three numbers to choose from.

To this day he doesn't remember how long he sat there in the silence, looking at the other three numbers. But his assistant had long since departed and night was falling as he went over and over the events in his mind.

One number was for The Third, now retired and currently residing in Bermuda. In his mind, he could hear his father's voice and already knew what he would say: "Never forget the faithful shareholders and Board members my boy. And what about those poor dear souls in Fahraysha, the ones we gave hope to. They stand to suffer greatly you know. They could lose it all."

The second number was for the Grimsby Police Station. A4 wasn't an expert in the law, but the fact the company had been convincing the world the E-THRILLA 3000 was safe, when it wasn't really, he couldn't help feeling there was serious trouble at the end of that phone number. It was the one that possibly worried him more than the others.

The third number was for Juan Kerr who, according to the Grimsby Gazette, was now overseas and working as a highly-paid consultant to various industries, including oil groups and fast-food corporations. Al knew that, if asked and paid the right way, Juan could come up with some devilishly clever plan. One that may not only extract the company from this crisis, but a plan that could save Al himself from a lifetime of shame.

Juan, the marketing magician, could no doubt make it all go away – for the company at least – and allow Al to make his own mark on the world. The one he'd been destined for all this time.

Al's office was a bleak, dark box from which there was no escape. As darkness crept over the carcass of the factory, his eyes registered the first stars starting to burst through the bluish, black velvet of the sky.

In the end, A4 said it wasn't about what he thought or even what he wanted. It came down to what he felt. What he felt deep down.

He picked up the phone.

Chapter 13

Defusing The Dominoes

Johnno Harrison later said the decision to phone the Grimsby Police station was the bravest thing that happened during the whole SLAKAR saga. It was the right thing to do, but it was the hardest thing to do – because it quite likely meant the end of a great family business and the end of a promising career, in an instant.

And the easiest thing for Al to do would have been to behave like a victim, because it hadn't really been his fault. But it was his responsibility.

While the Grimsby Police station may have taken the call, the matter was promptly taken over by the Government's Special Investigations Unit.

So rather than the police coming

around, the boss of The Box & All Company was surprised to receive a visit from the nation's top public servant Henry Stamper and LEADERS' leader Johnno Harrison. Al couldn't quite work out why they were the ones to appear, but he felt certain they would let him know his punishment soon enough. Despite his looming demise, he felt strangely calm and comfortable with his visitors and his fate.

As soon as Johnno and A4 shook hands they smiled, and remembered each other as young kids playing at the factory – all that time ago. They had grown a lot since then. But as they looked each other in the eye, they could just tell. Here was someone you could believe in.

What Johnno couldn't believe though, was what had pride of place on Al's desk – The Golden Orb – the trophy his Dad had made and painted in gold for the kids of the workers and managers. The one they used to play for at the old factory after school.

"Well, I did captain the last winning side," smiled Al, which prompted both of them to recall classic contests, characters and hilarious incidents of games gone by.

And as they brought each other up to date with what had been happening in the years since, they realised they knew many of the same people. The ones giving Al special training via computer were the same experts that Johnno had met on his recent travels across the country.

For it was true that both had been groomed to be leaders. Al for the family business, and Johnno by his circumstances. But leadership also requires something from within.

Both had made it through, partly, because they understood where they'd come from and, partly, because they were prepared to square up to a challenge. Recently promoted editor Ophelia Payne had even written a piece in the latest Grimsby Gazette, revealing Johnno was being sounded out as a future member of parliament, with a view to 'the top job down the track'.

For the moment though, it was Henry Stamper who manufactured a polite cough at the right time, and everyone immediately knuckled down to the issues at hand. Stamper got to the point.

"You've done the right thing Farquhar

and I know you're in a pickle, through no fault of your own, but I think we can see this right. Because, quite frankly the current government, and its likely replacement, are both in a pickle too. And that's what might see us clear in all this.

"As you know, the latest election is upon us and it looks quite certain I'm going to get some new bosses. The SLAKAR crisis and your secret report, implicating the E-THRILLA, are a serious business. Serious business indeed.

"But that's why I've asked Johnno along. I'll let him fill you in shortly, as I've got to get straight back to my office at Triplicate House on the next train.

Then the Chief Secretary said the words that came through to Al in waves. A kind of pulsing, magical, other-worldly echo.

"It's fair to say the LEADERS program is providing some *real hope* with the Syndrome ... with *healthy progress* now being recorded among the SLAKARS ... *No doubt about it ... The first good news in ages ...* but a bit late for my current masters."

Al was caught off guard to the point of feeling giddy, but quickly shook his head and snapped back in as Stamper continued.

"Thankfully the likely next government has had the very good sense to keep the scheme as an election policy priority. It's even linking it in with its *Bringing Our Jobs Back Home* campaign. So things may actually soon be looking up, in more ways than one old boy."

A4 – the doomed, the condemned, the shamed – could not quite believe what he was hearing. He wanted to fast forward the conversation to find out more detail, but also didn't want to miss a single word. He wasn't sure what the future held, but in an instant it seemed to be filling with hope and possibility, whereas moments before all he could see was a never-ending legacy of guilt and despair. A deep dark hole, but now light was bursting everywhere.

Henry Stamper went on to explain that the matter had been referred to the government's special investigations unit, because there were national (and global) concerns about the spread of SLAKAR Syndrome, as well as the lobbyist laws preventing criticism of people using the E-THRILLA 3000. He explained, though, that the good thing about rules is you can always make another one if you needed to.

Certainly the existing government was in deep, for it wasn't just taking donations from The Box & All Company for the children's hospital wards (through *The Box & All Wellness Foundation* Juan had set up with the Health Department). To complicate matters, the government had started *relying* on the foundation equipment, rather than providing its own funding for kids in hospitals. And that support, of course, was now officially linked to the global SLAKAR health crisis, which threatened to bring down other governments and economies around the world, as Henry Stamper described it, "Like crashing, exploding dominoes."

"So, it's a sticky wicket old boy. Quite frankly, we need to make things right without causing any unnecessary panic. And, sick kiddies aside, this isn't just political self-interest at play Farquhar. This whole caper is in the national interest and, whichever way you look at it, everyone's interest.

With his heart racing, his eyes wide with wonder, and his mouth half agape,

Al *almost* understood what Stamper was trying to say, and later admitted he almost fell through the floor (before wanting to rebound through the roof) when he heard what came next.

"And that's why we've got to get this Grimsby factory going again *fast.*"

Stamper saw a shocked look in Al Farquhar's face, like he'd been hit by a bolt of lightning. "Don't worry, we'll pay for the machines – just the old bat and ball machines mind you – to get moved back in, at no cost to you.

Henry then explained a key part of the deal. "The Fahraysha factory needs to keep making the computer game – with some important health modifications of course! I'll let Johnno here explain it all shortly.

"Good luck old boy – you've now got two factories to run and I have memos waiting to be fired off. Tally-ho chaps, exciting times ahead!"

And with that, Henry Stamper shook A4's hand, gave Johnno a quick nod, and rushed out of the room to catch the Grimsby Flyer back to the big city.

Chapter 14

Catching The Future

A4 looked at Johnno with a combination of disbelief, awe, and a strange half-smile on his face. Johnno smiled back and explained what Henry Stamper didn't have time to.

The LEADERS program had been an outstanding success. People were training themselves for the future they'd always wanted, and there were plenty of jobs that needed to be filled. Not just in Grimsby and across the country, but around the world.

But perhaps most importantly of all, the campaign to get the SLAKARS involved was having terrific results, and that was one of the reasons Johnno had been asked along to the meeting.

SLAKARS who had committed to the LEADERS program (after starting off with the OUT component) were getting a lot more than just exercise, laughter, new friends, and a new future.

They were getting taller.

Slowly, surely and painlessly, they were rising up. The theory from the Stealth Institute was correct. The Grimsby Gazette was already rushing out a special edition with the headline *SLAKARS BREAK-THROUGH REVEALED – THE LONG AND THE SHORT OF IT.*

Al's eyes suddenly welled up with tears, but he quickly caught himself as Johnno added, "It's great news, but we have a serious need to get this factory going again."

The LEADERS program had spread so far and so quickly, that there was now a chronic shortage of decent bats and balls – the old ones made at the Grimsby factory. The ones that lasted and the ones that were helping the SLAKARS (and everyone else) to get moving.

Because the company had bought and shut-down all its competitors, it was the only place still capable of making the bats and balls.

And the sporting gear was central to the games that a fully recovered Horrie, and an overjoyed Jenny, were now helping to run, as a crucial part of the LEADERS scheme. (As a matter of fact, a very chuffed Horrie had even dusted off the Quality Control Cup and it was being competed for on a national level.)

"Johnno, this is simply brilliant," Al beamed, almost choking his words.

"I mean, I know there's so much to be put right. My head's spinning at the moment and re-opening Grimsby will be like a dream come true for me, to have life back in this place again ...

And then he stopped. "But I'm afraid the company is still facing ruin." Suddenly, the excitement drained out of his face, with despair and dread cruelly flooding back.

"You see, all our money was ploughed into the launch of the BLACK MAX 4000 and it's been a marketing disaster."

Johnno nodded his head, leaned forward, and with his eyes smiling, put a hand on Al's shoulder. "I have some news on that front.

"I know you've been swamped with the findings from the Stealth Institute, but there have been things going on behind-the-scenes."

Concerns about the impending *Bringing Our Jobs Back Home* campaign had reached Fahraysha, prompting a lightning strike of factory and transport workers. They feared they were about to suffer the same fate as the retrenched Grimsby workers all those years before. As a result, the BLACK MAX 4000 shipments never made it out. And that's when Henry Stamper swooped.

He quickly established negotiations between the governments, so that everyone got the result they wanted. Each would have a factory, and the jobs that go with it.

In addition, a new international wages deal would be established, called 'The Grimsby Standard' (which workers throughout Fahraysha were rightly ecstatic about).

Stamper's team would pay for the old bat and ball machines to be re-established at Grimsby, at no expense to the company, and the Fahraysha government agreed to repackage and rebadge the new computer device as 'WHITE LIGHTNING' (pending approval from A4).

There would also be new heat-resistant

components, as well as radiation protection and reduced light flicker. Plus, games would be programmed to allow players to complete their missions in stages, set to a maximum of 90 minutes, rather than being forced to outlast their rivals by refusing to eat, sleep, move (or even go to the toilet).

Here Johnno paused. "That is, of course, if you agree. This is, after all, your company and your *two* factories. Henry just needs your go ahead."

Al looked back at Johnno with a strong, proud glint in his eye. "Where do I sign?"

The two young men then walked through the factory – as if in a dream – picturing the dark old hulk of a place back to its humming, bustling best.

They spoke about where the machines would go and the quantities of bats and balls that would need to be produced to meet global demand. They also kept interrupting each other with memories about things they'd seen happening at the factory in certain places. And as they got to the loading area, where the Quality Control Cup and the Golden Orb had been contested in such great spirit for so many years, Al found himself saying something as if by reflex or instinct:

"I'd like your Dad to come back. He was our heartbeat. Please, would you be so kind as to let me ask him myself, if you think that's OK."

With that, it was Johnno whose eyes started to get glassy. But then he snapped back into the moment, when Al added: "In fact, I want you and your Mum and the LEADERS program here as well. It's crucial."

Smiling, Johnno looked him in the eye. "I'm sure Mum and Dad will be thrilled. I've got a few things on my plate nowadays Al, but I will oversee this to make sure you have the very best people here."

They started to move on, but then the head of the rapidly expanding company stopped dead in his tracks, realising something that now seemed so obvious: "There are some people I need you to meet."

As they resumed walking through vast empty spaces, and up and down stairs that echoed loudly, Johnno spoke about the special new equipment SLAKAR converts were using on the LEADERS program.

The devices had been developed by Sir Rennie Tee. One was called the Elasta-tron and looked similar to a big pair of Wellington boots. It acted like suction caps on short legs.

Another device resembled an exercise bike with the games controller attached to the handlebars. It had a generator and a timer connected to the gears, with the user needing to pedal away to provide power to the E-THRILLA 3000. The cogs would automatically disconnect after a 90-minute session.

Sir Rennie had also been trying to patent a special wireless frequency which allowed the system to operate, but the signal was only activated at certain times of the day on a heavily discounted payment plan.

Johnno was about to tell him about even more inventions when he came to the research and development room. The place where SLAKARS were stacked high on their stools, in neat rows, playing and creating the very latest games for the all-new, improved device.

Al turned up the light – but not so fast as to startle them. And just enough for them to clearly see Johnno and himself.

"I have some wonderful news," he announced.

He went on to explain all the things that had happened and promised them their games development would continue at Grimsby, triggering a flurry of great relief and excitement.

A4 then introduced his 'good friend' to the group. But they already knew who he was, as many of their SLAKAR friends had joined the LEADERS program and, while those people didn't play games like they used to, they let everyone know how exciting things had become "on the outside".

Which is just as well, because it meant people didn't fear what might happen next – they could actually look forward to something of an adventure.

You could tell in the faces of the SLAKARS that it was OK. Whatever the future held, they had trust and confidence in the people standing before them. There was an incredible sense of anticipation and hope coursing through the room.

And so it was that – with a strong yet friendly face – Johnno Harrison began with the words long remembered around the great go-ahead town of Grimsby.

They came with a mix of power and

kindness, and a crack of electricity and excitement.

"*Friends – It's time! Time to stand up and catch the future!*"

And he was right.